# This book belongs to

_____

Based on the TV series *Nick Jr. The Backyardigans*™ as seen on Nick Jr.®

**SIMON SPOTLIGHT**
An imprint of Simon & Schuster Children's Publishing Division
1230 Avenue of the Americas, New York, New York 10020
*Race to the Tower of Power, Pirate Treasure, Secret Agents, Mission to Mars, Say "Please!", The Secret of Snow*, and *The Polka Palace Party* © 2006 Viacom International Inc. All rights reserved.
NICK JR., *Nick Jr. The Backyardigans*, and all related titles, logos, and characters are trademarks
of Viacom International Inc. NELVANA™ Nelvana Limited. CORUS™ Corus Entertainment Inc.
All rights reserved, including the right of reproduction in whole or in part in any form.
SIMON SPOTLIGHT and colophon are registered trademarks of Simon & Schuster, Inc.
Manufactured in the United States of America
4  6  8  10  9  7  5  3
ISBN-13: 978-1-4169-3842-2
ISBN-10: 1-4169-3842-7
These titles were previously published individually by Simon Spotlight.

# Big Book

## of Backyard Adventures

SIMON SPOTLIGHT / NICK JR.

New York   London   Toronto   Sydney

# Contents

# The Backyardigans

# Race to the Tower of Power

adapted by Catherine Lukas
based on the original teleplay by Adam Peltzman
illustrated by Dave Aikins

Pablo and Tyrone were playing in the backyard.

"Wa-ha-haa! We're supervillains!" said Pablo. "I'm Yucky Man. I have the power to make things yucky!"

"And I'm Dr. Shrinky!" said Tyrone. "I have the power to make things small! Wa-ha-haa!"

"Hey, Dr. Shrinky!" said Pablo. "Let's use our supervillain powers to take over the world!"

"Yeah!" replied Tyrone. "To do that, we need to capture the Key to the World that's hidden in the Tower of Power! Wa-ha-haa! Let's go!"

As soon as the villains left, two superheroes bounded into the yard.

"I'm Captain Hammer!" said Austin proudly. "I can build anything!"

"And I'm Weather Woman!" announced Uniqua. "I have the power to change the weather!"

"Look!" said Austin, pointing to a tiny, gooey slide. "The supervillains have been here!"

"They must be after the Key to the World," said Uniqua. "Come on. It's superheroes to the rescue!"

Meanwhile, Pablo and Tyrone were making villainous plans in the Forest of Darkness. . . .

"This way, Yucky Man!" said Tyrone. "We need to cross the Land of Cold!"

"Not so fast, supervillains," said a voice.
"Superheroes!" yelled Pablo.
The heroes chased after the villains.
"Ground . . . get sticky!" ordered Pablo.
ZLURP! The ground beneath the superheroes turned into a yucky, smelly mud pit.

"We're stuck!" cried Uniqua as she watched the villains escape. "Quick! Captain Hammer—get us out of here!"

Austin found a stone and banged it with his superhero hammer. Quick as a flash, a mud-sucking vacuum cleaner appeared and sucked up all the yucky mud.

"Come on!" called Uniqua. "We can't let the villains get to the Tower of Power before we do!"

17

"Brrr!" said Austin a few moments later. "I guess we've reached the Land of Cold."

"Look!" said Uniqua, pointing. The villains were sliding across the ice toward the Tower. "Quick! Build us a boat, Captain Hammer!"

BANG! Austin hit a twig with his toy hammer. . . .

And—POOF!—a boat appeared.

"And now I'll use my superpowers to change the weather!" said Uniqua. "Weather change—to hot!"

The sun grew hot. CRACK! The ice began to melt.

"Uh-oh!" said Tyrone. "The ice is melting!"

Moments later the two villains stood stranded on a tiny iceberg while the superheroes rowed past them.

Then Pablo had an idea. He pointed at the water.

"Superheroes hate yucky, smelly goo," he said. "Water—turn to gobbly-goo!"

ZLURF!

"Eeew!" said Uniqua. "I hate yucky goo!"

"You can't defeat the power of yuck!" Pablo shouted as the supervillains sloshed past.

"I know!" said Austin. "I'll build a bridge!" WHACK! went his hammer. Moments later the superheroes were running over a bridge and toward the Tower of Power.

"Drat!" said Pablo as the superheroes dashed past them. "Foiled again! Do something, Dr. Shrinky!"

Tyrone pointed at Austin and unleashed his shrinking rays. ZAP!

"We've got to get to the top first!" squeaked a tiny Austin as the villains ran into the Tower. "It's up to you, Weather Woman!"

Uniqua waved her arms. WHOOSH! A twister picked them up off the ground and carried them up, up, up to the top of the tower.

"At last!" said Pablo. "We've got the Key to the World!"
"Oh, no you don't!" shouted Uniqua.
As Tyrone and Pablo shot their rays at Uniqua, she grabbed
the key and held it up. . . .

The rays bounced off the key and back onto the villains, shrinking them and covering them with goo. Then Austin banged a paper clip with his hammer. The tiny, gooey villains found themselves trapped in a cage.

"Please let us out!" said Pablo. "We promise to be nice!"

"If we let you out," said Uniqua, "then you have to promise to be superheroes. And instead of stealing the Key to the World, promise that you'll help us protect it."

"We promise!" said Pablo and Tyrone.
Austin opened the door to the cage, and out they came.
Then Tyrone made all three of them big again.

"I'm not Dr. Shrinky anymore!" announced Tyrone. "I'm Dr. Grow, the superhero!"

"And I'm now . . . Very Clean Guy!" said Pablo. Suddenly they heard a rumbling sound.

"I'm also a very _hungry_ guy," Pablo said, laughing.

"Let's all go to my house for a supersnack," suggested Austin. "We have granola bars."

Before going into Austin's house, Pablo turned and looked at everyone.

"Wa-ha-haa!" he cackled. Uniqua looked at him sternly.

"Oops!" said Pablo. "I mean . . . superheroes to the rescue!"

# Pirate Treasure

35

adapted by Justin Spelvin
based on the original teleplay by McPaul Smith
illustrated by Matthew Stoddart

It was a perfect day for an adventure. Uniqua decided to be a pirate!

"Arrrr!" she said. "I'm Captain Uniqua."

She drew a big pirate flag in the sandbox.

"I'm Captain Austin with a hook for a hand!" Austin announced. He showed Uniqua his hook.

"Two pirates are better than one," said Uniqua. "Let's hunt for treasure together. I have half a treasure map, matey!"

"Arrrr!" Captain Austin answered. "Let's go!"

"Pirates!" Pablo said, pointing to the sand. "Pirates were here!"

"Can we be pirates too?" asked Tyrone. "I'll be Captain Tyrone with a wooden ear!"

"Arrrr!" said Pablo. "And I'm Captain Pablo with the peg leg!"
The two new pirates sailed their ship across the ocean.
"Arrrr! I see another ship," Tyrone called. "Let's raid it! That's what scurvy pirates do!"

Pablo and Tyrone climbed aboard the other ship and bumped right into Captain Uniqua and Captain Austin!

"Arrrr!" said Pablo. "Time to walk the plank."

"Hey, that sounds like fun!" said Uniqua. She and Austin jumped onto the plank with a laugh.

Uniqua and Austin walked off the plank . . . but they didn't splash into water. They landed in soft, soft sand!

"It's a desert island," said Uniqua. "Just like on our half of the treasure map!"

"We have half a treasure map too!" called Tyrone.
That gave Austin an idea.

"Maybe we should be one big band of pirates and put our halves of the map together," said Austin.

They put the two halves of the map together . . . and then they had a whole map!

"Look!" Uniqua said, pointing. "That *X* marks the spot where the treasure is buried."

The four pirates followed the map. They walked and walked.

Finally they came to a bubbling, stinky mud pit.

"It looks a little far to jump," said Austin.

"I think I see a way," said Uniqua. "We can walk across that tree."

"But I'm a peg-legged pirate," said Pablo. "Balancing is going to be tricky!"

Pablo took a small step. Then another. Then another. He was almost there!

But then he started to wobble. Pablo was going to fall!
"Arrrr!" cheered Tyrone. "You can do it!"

The three other pirates rushed over. They pulled Pablo to safety.
"Arrrr! Thanks, guys!" Pablo said.
"Arrrr! No problem," said the pirates.

The map said the *X* was nearby.
"I found a *V*," said Pablo.
"This one is a *W*," called Austin.
"Arrrr! Over here!" said Uniqua. "I found the *X*!"

They each took turns digging. Suddenly Uniqua hit something very hard.

"It's a treasure chest!" she called.
They pulled it out of the ground and opened the lid.

"It's the biggest diamond ever!" said Pablo.

"All in favor of sharing it, say 'Arrrr!'" said Uniqua.

"Arrrr!" cheered the pirates.

"But first let's bury it here," said Uniqua, "so that other pirates can't steal it."

"We can use the map to find it later," said Tyrone. "Let's mark the spot with a *Y*. No one will ever think of looking for a *Y*."

They quickly buried the treasure.

When the treasure was buried, the pirates stood and admired their work.

"All this pirating has made me hungry," said Uniqua. "All in favor of a snack, say 'Arrrr!'"

"Arrrr!" cheered Pablo, Austin, and Tyrone.

So the pirates headed home for a snack.

adapted by Wendy Wax
based on the original teleplay by McPaul Smith
illustrated by Zina Saunders

Pablo peeked out from behind a tree.

"Shh, I'm Agent Pablo—a *secret* agent. Secret agents go on secret missions!"

Tyrone crept out from behind a bush. "I'm Agent Tyrone!" he said.
"All clear, Agent Pablo?"
"All clear, Agent Tyrone!" said Pablo.

Just then Uniqua sneaked out from behind a bush.
"I'm Agent Uniqua," she said, "and I'm extremely sneaky!"

"What is our secret mission, Agent Pablo?" asked Tyrone.

Pablo held up a box with a bone inside it. "We need to sneak into the Treasure Museum to return this mystery bone to its secret owner," he said.

"Who's the secret owner?" asked Uniqua.

"I don't know," Pablo said. "It's a secret, but he's in the Treasure Museum."

"But the Treasure Museum has alarms and booby traps!" said Tyrone.

"Secret agents can *always* find a way to sneak in," said Uniqua.

Outside the Treasure Museum, Pablo showed the other agents his spy gadget. It was small with lots of top-secret buttons. Uniqua had brought a spy power rope to help them in tough situations. Tyrone had brought a bottle of maple syrup.

"Maple syrup!" said Pablo and Uniqua. "What's that for?"
"It's spy maple syrup," said Tyrone. "In case we need something sticky."

"Let's go," said Uniqua.

"Secret agents never just *go* in. They *sneak* in!" said Pablo. He used his spy gadget to open a secret trap door at their feet.

"How will we get down there?" asked Tyrone.
"No problem! With my spy power rope!" said Uniqua. "Grab on,
agents! We're going down!"

The secret agents found themselves in the Hall of Precious Jewels.

"Rubies, emeralds, and pearls!" said Tyrone. "These certainly are precious jewels."

"Watch out for alarms and booby traps in here," said Pablo.
"Look! This must be the biggest diamond in the world,"
Uniqua exclaimed, turning to her friends. But in her excitement,
she bumped into the stand that held the huge diamond.
"Watch out!" Pablo cried as the diamond fell.

Tyrone caught the
diamond—just as a cage
fell down from the ceiling.
*Clank!*

"Oh, no!" cried Uniqua.
"A booby trap!"

"We're trapped!" cried
Pablo, starting to panic.
"Uh-oh! Secret agents
should never get trapped.
But we're trapped.
Uh-oh . . ."

"Pablo!" said Uniqua. "Calm down. We have to be cool and think."
"We *could* try my spy maple syrup," suggested Tyrone.
"Nah," said Uniqua and Pablo.

"Maybe if we put the diamond back, the cage will go up," said Uniqua.
Pablo pressed a button on his spy gadget. A mechanical arm with
a claw grabbed the diamond and returned it to its base—and the cage
began to rise.

The agents came to a doorway. Three laser beams blocked their way.

"If we touch the laser beams, we'll set off an alarm!" warned Pablo.

"But how do we get past them?" asked Tyrone.

"We've got to do the limbo under the beams," said Pablo.

79

After they carefully went under the laser beams, the secret agents came upon the Gargantuan Gallery.

"How will we find the secret owner of the mystery bone?" Uniqua asked.

Just then she tripped over a dinosaur's foot. It was missing a baby toe.

"You found him!" said Pablo. "The mystery bone is the dinosaur's toe!"

"We need something sticky to attach the toe to the foot," said Uniqua.

"I *knew* my spy maple syrup would come in handy," said Tyrone. He stuck the bone in place. "Mission accomplished!"

"Let's get out of here!" said Tyrone.
Uniqua shot the spy power rope up through the skylight.
"Grab hold, agents!" she said. "Going up!"

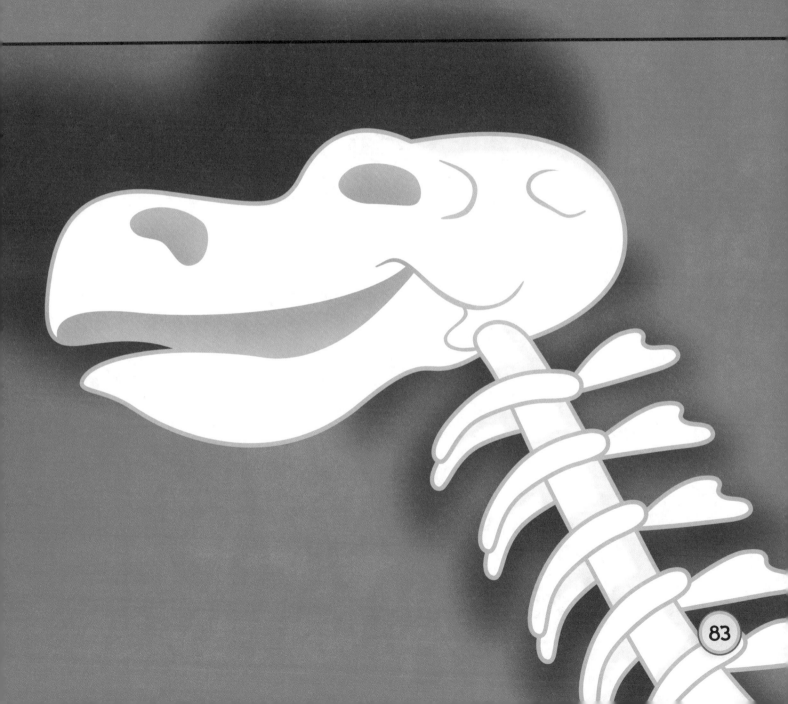

"That was quite a mysterious adventure!"
said Tyrone.
"And very sneaky," said Uniqua.
"Now let's have a snack at my house!"
So off they all went for a secret agent snack.

87

adapted by Wendy Wax
based on the original teleplay by Robert Scull
illustrated by Warner McGee

Uniqua, Pablo, and Austin were in the backyard.
"I'm Mission Commander Uniqua!" said Uniqua. "I'm getting ready
to lift off on a mission to Mars."
"I'm the astronaut in charge of science!" said Pablo.
"I'm in charge of all the equipment we're bringing with us," said
Austin.

"Mission Control here," Tyrone said to the astronauts. "We've been getting a strange signal from Mars. It goes: *'Boinga, boinga, boinga!'*"

"Space shuttle crew, we need you to find out what's making that noise," said Tasha.

"Affirmative!" said Commander Uniqua.

"Good luck, astronauts," said Tyrone. "We'll communicate with you from Earth."

"Roger that, Mission Control. Space shuttle ready for liftoff!" reported Commander Uniqua.

Tyrone counted down. "Five . . . four . . . three . . . two . . . one! Lift off to Mars!"

Up, up, up went the space shuttle, past the moon and around the stars.

"I see Mars!" cried Pablo.

"It's really red!" said Commander Uniqua. "Mission Control, we're approaching Mars and ready for landing!"

"Congratulations, shuttle crew!" said Yasha from Mission Control. "You're the first astronauts to go to Mars!"

"Here, boy!" Austin called into the space shuttle.

R.O.V.E.R., a six-wheeled vehicle with a robotic arm, appeared. He was loaded down with important supplies.

"With all this equipment, we're ready for anything," said Austin.

"Listen, Commander!" said Tasha from Mission Control. "We're getting that signal again!"

*Boinga, boinga, boinga!* came over the two-way radio.

"Find out where the noise is coming from, shuttle crew," said Tyrone.

"Roger!" said Commander Uniqua. They climbed aboard R.O.V.E.R. and set off.

"Look out!" cried Pablo. "It's a meteor shower!"

"It's a good thing we're ready for anything," said Austin. He pressed a button and a space umbrella popped out of R.O.V.E.R.'s trunk. The meteors bounced right off the space umbrella!

"We're having a small meteor shower," Uniqua reported to Mission Control.

Suddenly giant meteors started to fall around the astronauts.

"Shuttle crew, seek shelter at once!" ordered Tyrone. "I repeat: Seek shelter!"

The astronauts ducked into a cave and found themselves on the edge of a cliff.

"I wonder how far down it goes," said Commander Uniqua.

"It's a long way down," said Pablo.

"Then let's head back," said Commander Uniqua. "We don't want to lose contact with Mission Control."

But before they could go anywhere, the ledge cracked and broke off. "*AHHH!*" cried Commander Uniqua, Pablo, and Austin as they tumbled down into darkness.

Down, down, down went the astronauts. Finally they landed with a splash in an underground lake.

"We lost R.O.V.E.R.!" cried Austin.

"We'll find him, Austin," said Commander Uniqua. "We're ready for anything, remember?" Then she tried to call Mission Control. All she got was static.

Meanwhile, Tyrone and Tasha were getting static too.
"Our astronauts are lost forever on Mars!" Tyrone said sadly.
"But they're ready for anything!" Tasha reminded him.

"We're on a mission!" Commander Uniqua reminded her fellow astronauts. "Astronauts never give up. Follow me."

They began hopping from rock to rock—until there were no more rocks.

"Now what do we do?" asked Pablo.

Suddenly they saw a trail of bubbles in the water.

"What is *that*?" Austin asked.

Just then R.O.V.E.R. popped out of the water!

"R.O.V.E.R.!" shouted Austin. "You can swim!" The astronauts climbed aboard and headed toward the distant shore.

On the shore was an underground city.

"Martians live here!" said Commander Uniqua. "Let's take a closer look."

The astronauts left R.O.V.E.R. and climbed up a stairway that led to a house.

They rang the doorbell. A little martian opened the door!
"*Boinga!*" the martian said with a giggle.
"'*Boinga*' must mean 'hello'!" Austin said with excitement. They followed the little martian inside.

The martian picked up the phone and dialed a number. Then she handed the phone to Commander Uniqua. The martian had called Tyrone at Mission Control!

"Tyrone!" shouted Commander Uniqua. "We found out what's making that sound! It's a martian, and she's been calling you this whole time."

"Amazing!" said Tyrone. "What's her name?"

"What's your name?" Commander Uniqua asked the little martian.

"*Boinga!*" replied the little martian.

"My name is Uniqua," said Commander Uniqua.

"*Boinga*, Uniqua!" said the little martian.

"You sure say '*boinga*' a lot," said Pablo.

"We say '*boinga*' for almost everything!" said the little martian.

Suddenly a giant martian appeared from the shadows.
"*Boinga*, Mommy!" said the little martian.
"*Boinga*, honey," said the mommy martian. "*Boinga*, earthlings. I'm afraid we have to go to bed. But please come back any time."

"We will!" said Uniqua.
Then Uniqua picked up the phone and spoke to Mission Control.
"Mission accomplished!" Uniqua announced. "What's next?"
"Return to Earth!" said Tasha. "It's time for a snack!"

109

Austin, Uniqua, and Pablo met up with Tyrone and Tasha in the backyard.

"That was a very martian-y adventure," said Tyrone.

"It sure was!" said Uniqua. "*Boinga, boinga, boinga!*"

"*Boinga, boinga, boinga!*" shouted the others as they ran inside for a snack.

NICK JR.

The BACKYARDIGANS

# Say "Please!"

## A Book About Manners

adapted by Catherine Lukas
based on the original teleplay by Janice Burgess
illustrated by Zina Saunders

"It is I, Princess CleoTasha of ancient Egypt," said Tasha. "It's great to have a big palace and servants who wait on me. Hey! Where *are* my servants, anyway?"

Princess CleoTasha clapped her hands. "Servant Tyrone! Servant Pablo! Servant Austin! Time to wait on me!"

The three loyal royal servants hurried over to her. "I'm thirsty," she said. "Bring me a glass of water!"

"But there is no water, O Princess," said Pablo. "The Nile River has dried up."

"Well, fill it back up!" said the princess.

"Only you can, O Princess," said Austin. "You must ask Sphinx Uniqua to tell you the secret of the Nile. Only then will the water return."

"But first you must bring her three presents. They are hidden all over Egypt," said Tyrone.

"And we'll help you find them," said Austin.

Princess CleoTasha and her loyal royal servants set off to find the presents.

"There's just one thing about Princess CleoTasha," said Pablo.

"She never says 'please,'" whispered Tyrone.

"Or 'thank you,'" mumbled Austin.

"What's the first present for the sphinx, Servant Tyrone?" asked Princess CleoTasha.

"It's called the Jewel of the Waters," answered Tyrone. "It is found inside the Hidden Pyramid."

They walked and walked and finally stopped in the Valley of the Pyramids. Then they noticed Servant Tyrone was leaning against something . . . something that they couldn't even see! It was the Hidden Pyramid! *Swish!* A door opened up.

Princess CleoTasha made Servant Tyrone go in first.
"Here it is, Princess," he said, pointing to a gleaming jewel.

"I found it!" the princess yelled, grabbing the huge jewel.
"The first present for the sphinx." She handed it to Tyrone. "It's heavy.
You carry it," she ordered him.

"She never says 'please,' " he murmured to himself.

"Okay, what's the second present, Servant Pablo?" asked the princess.

"It's the yellow lotus flower that grows on the Cliffs of Karnak," said Pablo.

"Let's get going," she ordered. "And don't forget my stuff."

The three loyal royal servants sighed. Once again she had forgotten to say "please" and "thank you."

After a long journey, they arrived at the Cliffs of Karnak.

"How am I supposed to get all the way up there?" asked the princess.

"The stairs, O Princess," Pablo explained.

"You go first," she ordered.

Servant Pablo shook his head. Once again she had not asked nicely.

Up, up, up they climbed. At the top of the cliff was a beautiful meadow filled with colorful lotus flowers.

Suddenly Servant Pablo spotted the only yellow flower and pointed to it.

"Oh! The yellow lotus flower! I found it!" the princess cried. She plucked the flower and handed it to Pablo. "You carry it. I have to walk down all those stairs."

"So do I," Pablo said quietly as he followed her down the stairs.

"Behold, I found the second present for the sphinx!" announced the princess as she reached the bottom of the cliff. "Two presents down, one to go. Where to next?"

"To get the third present we must travel to the Secret Oasis," said Austin.

"Remind me, what's an oasis?" asked the princess.

"It's a green place with trees and water in the middle of the desert," Austin replied.

"Let's get that last present now," ordered the princess. "And don't forget my stuff."

The three loyal royal servants were all thinking the same thing: She forgot to say "please" again.

They all walked and walked until they reached the Secret Oasis.
"The third present is a drink of water from the Secret Oasis," said
Austin, handing the princess a golden cup.

"Great! I've got the third present!" the princess cheered. She scooped up the crystal-clear water and handed it to Servant Austin. "You carry it," she demanded. "Now that I have all three presents, it's time to go talk to that sphinx! Let's go, my loyal royal servants. To Sphinx Uniqua!"

They traveled through the desert along the dried-up banks of the Nile. At last they saw Sphinx Uniqua.

"Greetings, Sphinx Uniqua," said the princess. "I am the Royal Princess CleoTasha, and I have brought you three presents. They are the Jewel of the Waters, the yellow lotus flower, and a golden cup of water from the Secret Oasis."

"Thank you so much!" said Sphinx Uniqua. "What lovely presents! Did you get them all by yourself?"

"Of course not, O Sphinx," replied the princess. "My loyal royal servants helped me. And they carried all my stuff."

"I see. Did you say 'thank you' for all of their help?" Sphinx Uniqua asked.

"Well, no," said the princess. "But will you tell me the secret of the Nile so there will be water in Egypt again?"

"Okay," replied the sphinx.

"The secret to almost everything is to always say 'please' and 'thank you.' You can start by saying 'thank you' to your servants who did all the work for you," whispered Sphinx Uniqua to the princess.

The princess looked surprised. Then she turned to her servants.

"Thank you for helping me and for doing all of the work," she said nicely.

"You're welcome!" said all three of them together.

"And thank you, O Sphinx, for telling me the secret of the Nile," Princess CleoTasha said.

"You're welcome," said the Sphinx.

And just like that, the Nile River began filling back up with water.

Everyone cheered!

"And now won't you all *please* join me for a snack?" Tasha asked them politely.

"Thank you! We'd love to!" said everyone else.

And they all went back to Tasha's house for a snack.

NICK JR

# The BACKYARDIGANS

# The Secret of Snow

139

adapted by Alison Inches
based on the original teleplay by Jonny Belt and Robert Scull
illustrated by Dave Aikins

Once upon a time there was a little girl who loved snow very much. "I love to sled!" she cried. "I love to catch snowflakes on my tongue! And I love to make snow angels!"

The only problem was that it wasn't snowing. So the little girl decided to try to discover the secret of snow by finding the Ice Lady, who lived far away in the Icy North. Surely the Ice Lady could make it snow!

The little girl set off for the Icy North—a cold, unfriendly place with gloomy, gray skies as far as the eye could see.

The Ice Lady and her assistant were hard at work making the world as icy as possible. The Ice Lady took her job very seriously. She had no time for rest or play, so when she spotted the little girl at her door, she became angry.

"No time for visitors!" she shouted. "To make the world nice, we need to fill it up with ice!"

Then the Ice Lady cranked a wheel on her control panel and sent the little girl swirling in a cyclone of ice cubes all the way . . .

. . . into the middle of a dry, sandy desert.

"Whew!" said the little girl. "How did I get here?"

"Howdy, ma'am!" shouted a passing cowboy. "I'm Cowboy Pablo,
and we need to get out of the way of that yonder twister!"

A tornado roared straight toward the little girl and Cowboy Pablo. It chased them to the left and to the right—and then cornered them against a rock wall!

"Well, ma'am," said Cowboy Pablo, "it looks like we're goners."

The Ice Lady's assistant, who had been watching the little girl and Cowboy Pablo from the Ice Factory, could see they needed help.
"I'll freeze the twister with the ice machine!" he cried.
He pushed a button on the control panel, and the twister froze solid.

"Tarnation!" cried Cowboy Pablo. "Is that snow?"

"No," said the little girl. "It's ice. Snow is lighter and fluffier and fun to play in."

Pablo liked the sound of snow, so the two new friends headed north to find the Ice Lady and the secret of snow.

When the Ice Lady saw them coming, she grew annoyed again. "Oh, for the love of ice!" she cried. "We don't need friendly visitors! We have *work* to do!"

Again she cranked a wheel on her control panel, and in a swirl of ice cubes she sent the little girl and Cowboy Pablo tumbling all the way . . .

151

. . . into a hot, steamy jungle. They landed on the vine of Tyrone of the Jungle. The vine dangled over a deep gorge.

"Gee," said Tyrone of the Jungle, "I wish I could rescue you, but this vine is about to break."

As the rope gave way, the Ice Lady's assistant, who had been watching everything, turned the waterfall into an icy slide. The friends slid to safety.

Then the little girl told her new friend all about her journey. Tyrone of the Jungle loved the sound of snow, so he joined the others on their trip back to the Icy North.

When the friends returned to the Ice Factory, the Ice Lady became madder than ever. She switched on her ice machine and froze everything inside her factory. The children—and the Ice Lady's assistant—tried to escape, but they slipped on the ice and slid onto the factory floor.

"No more interruptions!" boomed the Ice Lady. "Now you will make ice for me! Get to work!"

But the friends found they liked to make ice—and this did not please the Ice Lady one bit. Ice making was serious business. The madder she got, the faster she cranked her ice machine. It went berserk, and her office filled up with ice.

"Help!" she screamed.

The Ice Lady's workers rushed to her office and pulled her out of the ice.
"You saved me!" said the Ice Lady with great surprise.
"Of course we did!" said the Ice Lady's assistant.
"That's what friends are for!" said the little girl.

"We didn't mean to interrupt your work," the little girl went on. "We just wanted to find out the secret of snow."

"I'm sorry," said the Ice Lady, who looked quite humbled. "But I don't know the secret of snow."

The little girl felt awful. Now it wasn't going to snow, and she had let down her friends. On top of that, she had disrupted the Ice Lady. "I'm so sorry," said the little girl glumly.

"When you've got good friends," said the Ice Lady, "who cares about snow?"

And just then, as if by magic, it began to snow.

And so Tyrone of the Jungle and Cowboy Pablo got their wish to see snow for the first time. And the little girl got to play in the backyard with all of her friends!

# The Polka Palace Party

## An Adventure in Teamwork

adapted by Erica David
based on the teleplay by McPaul Smith
illustrated by Warner McGee

Tyrone strolled out into the sunshine.

"Howdy," he said. "I'm Cowboy Tyrone, and this here is my trusty tuba."

Tyrone blew into his tuba and played a polka tune. "That's a mighty purty sound," he said happily.

167

"I'm going to a surprise birthday party with my friend Sherman the Worman," explained Cowboy Tyrone. "The party is for Sherman's brother, and it's at the Polka Palace in Wyoming. I'm going to play my tuba so all the Wormans can dance the polka."

"We've got quite a ways to go to get to Wyoming," continued Cowboy Tyrone. "Come on, Sherman. Let's make tracks!"

Sherman the Worman and Cowboy Tyrone were moseying on their way to the Polka Palace when they heard a voice call out for help. It was a cowgirl, and she was in trouble!

"Hang on, pardner!" called Cowboy Tyrone.

Cowboy Tyrone ran to catch the cowgirl, who slipped from the branch and fell right into his tuba.

"Thanks, amigo!" the cowgirl exclaimed. "And thanks to your tuba, too!"

The cowgirl dusted herself off.

"Howdy!" she said. "I'm Cowgirl Uniqua. Now, where is my clarinet?"

"There it is," Cowboy Tyrone exclaimed.

"Thank goodness!" said Cowgirl Uniqua. "Without my clarinet, I couldn't play my favorite kind of music—the polka."

"The polka?" Cowboy Tyrone cried. "That's my favorite music too!"
Cowboy Tyrone invited Cowgirl Uniqua to come play polka music at
the Polka Palace.

173

Cowgirl Uniqua, Sherman the Worman, and Cowboy Tyrone made tracks across the great open plain.

Suddenly a group of horses thundered into their path. Then another cowboy came galloping after the horses.

"Help!" Cowboy Pablo shouted. "Runaway horses!"

"Don't worry," said Cowboy Tyrone. "If we all work together, we can stop them!"

Cowgirl Uniqua helped Cowboy Pablo open the gate to the corral. Then Cowboy Tyrone blew into his tuba with all his might. To everyone's amazement the horses stopped in their tracks and headed into the corral.

"Runaway horses always stop running when they hear a tuba," Cowboy Tyrone explained.

"Good thinking!" Cowgirl Uniqua said. "That was mighty fine teamwork, pardners."

"Thanks, y'all," Cowboy Pablo said. "Now it's feeding time."

Cowboy Pablo picked up an accordion and played a feeding-time song for the horses.

"That music sure sounds purty," said Cowgirl Uniqua.
"It's my favorite kind of music—the polka," Cowboy Pablo replied.
Cowboy Tyrone and Sherman the Worman decided that Cowboy Pablo should come play with them at the Polka Palace too.

At last the cowboys came to a mighty river.
"Look, a cowboy on a raft!" Cowboy Pablo said.

"Howdy," called Cowboy Tyrone. "We're going to a polka party. Could you give us a ride?"

"Sure, pardners," said Cowboy Austin.

"Say, are those your drums?" asked Cowgirl Uniqua.

"They sure are. I like to play the polka on them," Cowboy Austin replied.

"You play the polka too?" Cowboy Tyrone asked.
"You should come play at the Polka Palace with us," said Cowboy Pablo.
That gave Cowboy Tyrone an idea. . . .

"Four instruments are better than one!" Cowboy Tyrone exclaimed. "Together we could have a polka band."

"That's a great idea!" Cowgirl Uniqua cheered.
"Uh-oh, amigos. There's trouble ahead," Cowboy Pablo warned them.
They were headed right for a waterfall!

The cowboys worked together to lasso a tree branch.
Then they helped one another climb from the raft to safety—but there wasn't time to save their instruments. The cowboys shook their heads sadly as they watched the instruments plunge over the waterfall.

"Our instruments are gone, but I'm glad you're here, pardners," said Cowboy Pablo.

"We make a great team, amigos, " Cowboy Tyrone agreed. "And we can still make it to the Polka Palace for the party."

At the Polka Palace the cowboys found a surprise waiting for them.
"Our instruments!" Cowgirl Uniqua cried.
"The Wormans must have found them in the river and brought them here!" Cowboy Austin exclaimed. "Strong little fellers!"

Just then Sherman's brother arrived.

"Surprise!" yelled the polka band.

"I know just how to thank the Wormans for finding our instruments," said Cowboy Tyrone.

The cowboys picked up their instruments and began to play a polka song.

The Wormans danced and cheered.

When the song was finished, Cowboy Tyrone's tummy rumbled.
"I think it's time for a snack," he said.
"That's music to my ears," Cowgirl Uniqua agreed.
So the cowboys strolled on home for feeding time.